Bonaparte

MARSHA WILSON CHALL

illustrations by

WENDY ANDERSON HALPERIN

DK Ink

DORLING KINDERSLEY PUBLISHING, INC.

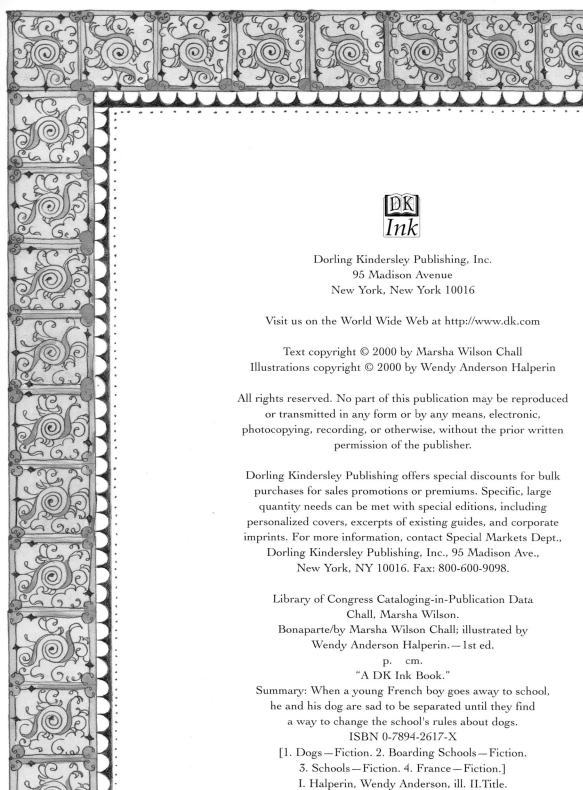

DK
Ink

Dorling Kindersley Publishing, Inc.
95 Madison Avenue
New York, New York 10016

Visit us on the World Wide Web at http://www.dk.com

Dorling Kindersley Publishing offers special discounts for bulk
purchases for sales promotions or premiums. Specific, large
quantity needs can be met with special editions, including
personalized covers, excerpts of existing guides, and corporate
imprints. For more information, contact Special Markets Dept.,
Dorling Kindersley Publishing, Inc., 95 Madison Ave.,
New York, NY 10016. Fax: 800-600-9098.

Library of Congress Cataloging-in-Publication Data
Chall, Marsha Wilson.
Bonaparte/by Marsha Wilson Chall; illustrated by
Wendy Anderson Halperin.—1st ed.
p.   cm.
"A DK Ink Book."
Summary: When a young French boy goes away to school,
he and his dog are sad to be separated until they find
a way to change the school's rules about dogs.
ISBN 0-7894-2617-X
[1. Dogs—Fiction. 2. Boarding Schools—Fiction.
3. Schools—Fiction. 4. France—Fiction.]
I. Halperin, Wendy Anderson, ill. II.Title.
PZ7.C3496 Bo 2000   [E]—dc21   00-021282

Book design by Annemarie Redmond.
The illustrations for this book were created in pencil
and watercolor.
The text of this book is set in 15 point Cochin.
Printed and bound in U.S.A.

First Edition, 2000
2 4 6 8 10 9 7 5 3 1

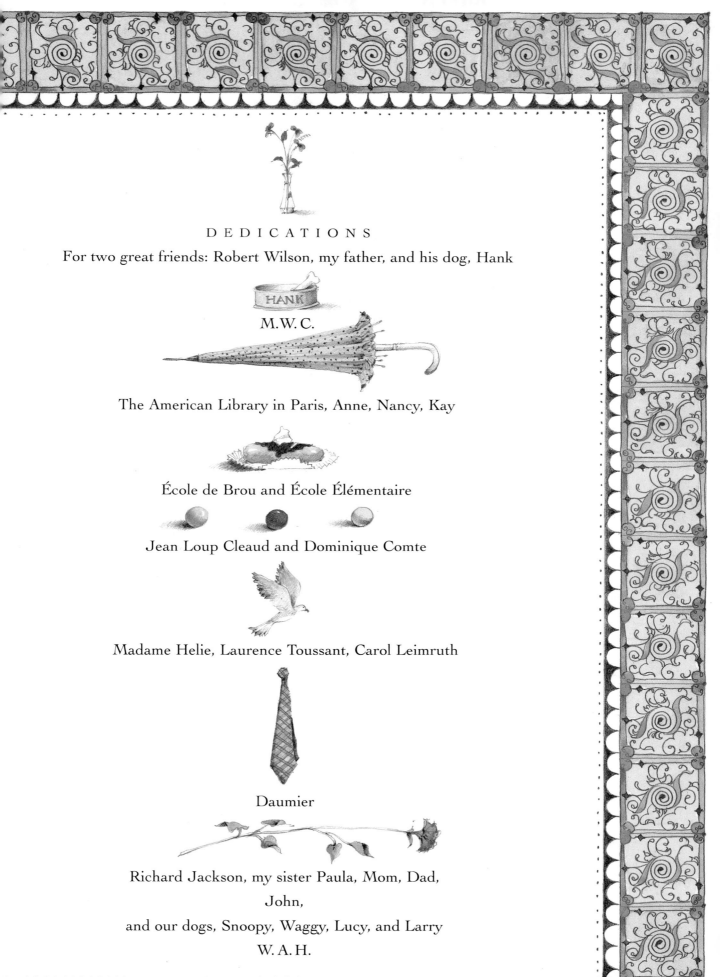

DEDICATIONS

For two great friends: Robert Wilson, my father, and his dog, Hank

M.W.C.

The American Library in Paris, Anne, Nancy, Kay

École de Brou and École Élémentaire

Jean Loup Cleaud and Dominique Comte

Madame Helie, Laurence Toussant, Carol Leimruth

Daumier

Richard Jackson, my sister Paula, Mom, Dad,
John,
and our dogs, Snoopy, Waggy, Lucy, and Larry

W. A. H.

The day they took Jean Claude away to school with his tuba, valise, and toy boat, they left Bonaparte at the château.

"Bonaparte!" the boy cried.

"You have everything you need, Jean Claude. Come along," the parents said. "Bonaparte, stay!" they ordered the dog. "No *dogs* at La School d'Excellence."

But the dog escaped the village to the streets of Paris, determined to find his boy.

Alone late that night on a pillow of stone, Bonaparte longed for the warm lap where he'd sprawled, lumpy and baggy with ease. He dreamed of Jean Claude in a window, calling, his words too small to hear.

Monday morning, Bonaparte followed Jean Claude's trail all the way to La School d'Excellence. "Good day," he said to the registrar. "I have come to fetch my boy, Jean Claude Jean."

"Impossible," said the registrar. "Discharges only to parents and guardians. Please refer to our sign."

Bonaparte did. And it said No Dogs Allowed.

On Tuesday, Bonaparte arrived disguised as a mother. "Sir," he said, his voice now higher, "I have come to visit my son, Jean Claude Jean."

"Just a moment," the registrar said, and surveyed the mother from hat to gloves.

"Your identification, please."

"But of course," answered Bonaparte in a ladylike way, and displayed his license.

"'Number one, two, three,'" the registrar read. "'If found, return to Jean Claude Jean, Rue de France, in the village of Montrouge.' Aha!" the man cried. "This is a *dog* license. I am no fool. Be off with you."

Wednesday, Bonaparte appeared as a student. "I would like to apply for admission to La School d'Excellence."

The registrar led him to the Regents' office for an application.

"We accept only the very best of all boys and girls,"
the Regents told him. "You must meet our exacting standards.
First, you will undergo a thorough health examination."

The doctor declared Bonaparte in perfect health.

The Regents keenly reviewed his report. "Clear eyes, cold nose, clean paws, straight tail. Healthy dog. Signed, Dr. Weissman."

"What? A *dog*!" the Regents shouted. "Thank goodness for the doctor's discovery, or we might have admitted this hound."

"Excuse me," the dog said, pressing his paw to his chest. "I am Bonaparte, as in Napoleon, the Emperor. Your sign says EQUAL OPPORTUNITY SCHOOL."

"But our first sign says NO DOGS ALLOWED. Students, parents, and staff only," the Regents said.

"Farewell, Bonaparte."

Thursday, from the band room, school drums *ba-da-boomed*.
Flutes ran scales, *toola-woo*. While the rest of the players
were heading for their places, a new drummer settled into the
percussion section. He kept watch for Jean Claude, but heard
no *oompah* from a tuba. When the band struck up a stirring
march, the drummer's tail wagged in four-quarter time.

"A *dog*!" the band leader cried.

Discovered again, Bonaparte fled without hearing a note from his boy.

Friday noon, the cafeteria lunch ladies served steaming leg of lamb. In hairnet and apron, the new lunch lady searched the line for Jean Claude.

"Bon appétit!" he remembered to say sixty-two times in a lunch-lady way. But never to Jean Claude, a boy who loved lamb nearly as much as Bonaparte did.

Duties at last complete, Bonaparte dined at the lunch-lady table. He ate heartily, like the other lunch ladies. Well, almost like the other lunch ladies.

"You *dog*!" they yelled, and Bonaparte ran, almost running out of hope.

But on Saturday morning, in the quiet dormitory, a new janitor mopped and dusted, occasionally sniffing for Jean Claude's bed.

The Regents found it first.

"Empty! Jean Claude has not slept here."

"The boy has run away!"

"He will be cold and hungry. We must find him before it's too late!"

Bonaparte threw down his broom. "So, my Jean Claude is missing!"

The Regents turned as one.

"That *dog*!"

"A dog?"

"A *dog*!"

And Bonaparte said, "At your service, gentlemen. Perhaps you need a dog to find him."

Nose to the trail, Bonaparte bounded out of the city,

ran through forests, jumped farmers' cobbled walls. He tracked village paths and alleys till a voice called, "Bonaparte!"

Could it be Jean Claude? Yes, yes! The dog felt it in his fur.

They nuzzled, danced, and tumbled. Bonaparte cried under the wide, clear sky, "Jean Claude, at last I have found you!"

"But I wasn't lost," Jean Claude told him,
"only on my way home to find *you*!"

Back at school, Jean Claude faced the Regents. "I will remain at La School d'Excellence only if the best of friends are admitted, too." He patted Bonaparte's head.

"Let's shake on it, gentlemen," the dog said. And what else could the Regents do?

From that day on at La School d'Excellence, the sign read N<u>ow</u> Dogs Allowed.

They arrived by air, on the train, via coach —
in balloon baskets, satchels, and arms.

La School d'Excellence would never be the same.
Classrooms panted and howled and woofed.

Meals, agreed the Regents, had clearly gone to the dogs.

By day, Bonaparte stretched his mind and caught flying objects of every kind.

And by night, he sprawled in warm laps, lumpy and baggy with ease, then curled round the feet of the boy he loved best, Jean Claude.

BONNE NUIT